About the Author

Brunilda Bonilla is a practicing attorney in New Jersey. She specializes in family and matrimonial law for more than twenty years. She is passionate about helping families navigate not only the legal system, but those important issues that touch upon and impact families, particularly those relationships between parents and children. She lives in Tenafly, New Jersey with her husband, Larry, three daughters, Emma, Claudia and Julianna, and tuxedo cat, Pepper.

Blue

Brunilda Bonilla

Blue

Nightingale Books

A CIP catalogue record for this title is
available from the British Library.

ISBN 9781838751456

Nightingale Books is an imprint of
Pegasus Elliot MacKenzie Publishers Ltd.
www.pegasuspublishers.com

First Published in 2022

Nightingale Books
Sheraton House Castle Park
Cambridge England

Printed & Bound in Great Britain

Dedication

I would like to dedicate *Blue* to my daughters, Emma, Claudia and Julianna, who have dared to do good in this world, and to all the children who feel sad sometimes.

Acknowledgements

I would like to thank my family for their love and support and my mom for always believing in me.

There was once a little boy who was always blue. Unlike other children, he often played alone. He felt lonely and sad, and wished things were different.

He lived in a world where everything was blue. Every morning when he looked out of his window, all he saw was blue – blue trees, blue houses, and even a blue school.

Inside his house, his room was blue. His bed was blue, his blanket a shade darker, and the rug beneath him a blue that was neither too dark nor too light. Little blue boy wished day and night he weren't so blue.

At school, the other kids would tease him because his shoulders stooped a little inward when he walked, and his voice was barely audible when he spoke.

He sat alone, ate alone, and played alone, trapped in all the blue around him until…

One day on his way back home from school he decided to go to some nearby woods. There, he stumbled across a butterfly lying on the ground right near his foot and almost imperceptible. It appeared that she had a broken wing.

Not knowing exactly what to do, he simply looked at her. Seeing that she could not pick herself up, the little boy gently lifted her up and placed her on a tree branch high above his head. In this way passersby, both human and animal alike, would not trample on her.

The butterfly sat there quietly for a few minutes before she spoke. Then she said, "Thank you, kind sir, for helping me up and placing me here, high above and away from the dangers below. But this is not where I belong. I was meant to fly and so I will. But before I do, please tell me how can I repay you for your kindness?"

Little blue boy, believing that the butterfly too could help him, and wanting nothing more in the world but to be happy, asked if she could help him turn his world into color. She looked at him lovingly and smiled. "Look around, my dear friend, and tell me what you see," she said calmly.

But just then, the skies quickly turned bitterly grey and it began to rain. He sat on the forest floor and cried, no longer able to tell apart the rain from his tears, as they streamed down his long, sad face.

"What now?" he asked in exasperation.

"Look around some more, boy," the butterfly said as she flapped her one wing. However, all the boy could see was nothing more than dreary, grey skies.

"Just look around a little more," she again insisted. And just as the boy was lifting his head, there in the distance, he saw a beautiful rainbow across the grey skies.

To this, the little boy's heart leapt with joy, for he was not only able to see the rainbow, but all the wonderful, beautiful, and vibrant colors all around him.

The butterfly noticed that the little blue boy was now standing a little taller and that his joy resounded throughout the forest because, you see, he too noticed that he was standing taller and that like the butterfly, he was meant to fly.

Without a moment's hesitation, the butterfly then asked the little boy to come closer, and as the boy reached up to the butterfly, she whispered in his ear, "My boy, go out into the world and do well for yourself, but once you have done well, go and do good." To this the butterfly smiled and added, "And as long as you do good, you will always have a rainbow."

And so by listening to the butterfly's wise words the boy went off and did a lot of good in the world... and was very, very happy.

CPSIA information can be obtained
at www.ICGtesting.com
Printed in the USA
BVHW020725210222
629615BV00020B/407

9 781838 751456